I SPY
TREASURE HUNT

A BOOK OF
PICTURE
RIDDLES

Photographs by Walter Wick

Riddles by Jean Marzollo

Cartwheel
·B·O·O·K·S·®

SCHOLASTIC INC.
New York   Toronto   London   Auckland   Sydney
Mexico City   New Delhi   Hong Kong

For Furlow, Chadwick, and Richard Word

W. W.

For Jennifer and Michelle Cotennec

J.M.

Book design by Carol Devine Carson

Go to www.scholastic.com for Web site information
on Scholastic authors and illustrators.

Library of Congress Cataloging-in-Publication Data

Wick, Walter.
    I spy treasure hunt: a book of picture riddles / photographs by Walter Wick; riddles by
Jean Marzollo.
        p.   cm.
    Summary: Rhyming verses ask readers to find hidden objects in the photographs.
    ISBN 0-439-04244-5
    1. Picture puzzles—Juvenile literature. [1. Picture puzzles.] I. Marzollo, Jean. II. Title.
GV1507.P47W5296   1999
793.73—dc21   99-30581
                                                                                 CIP

20   19 18 17 16 15 14   02 03 04

Printed in Mexico   49
First printing, September 1999

TABLE OF CONTENTS

Picture riddles fill this book;
Turn the pages! Take a look!

Use your mind, use your eye;
Read the riddles — play I SPY!

I spy a sea horse, a thumbtack, a cone,

Scissors, a dolphin, a spoon, TELEPHONE;

A penny, a dog, and a rolling pin,
A hanger, a hatchet, and DUCK POND INN.

Standing on the porch of Duck Pond Inn,
I spy two coins, and a lazy clothespin;

Three dogs, two fishhooks, a broken oar,
A needle, a spool, and the TREASURE CHEST store.

I spy a dime, two dolphins, a tub,

Ten bowling pins, and a little golf club;

Two fishing poles, a leaning mousetrap,
A snowflake, a crab, two bats, and a map.

I spy three anchors, a small cannonball,
Five horses, a noose, and the word WATERFALL;

A shovel, a shark, two ships at port,
A bell, a boot, a mermaid, and FORT.

Standing in the fort and looking at the view,

I spy three ducks, a paintbrush, too;

A tortoise, a hare, a tea bag, a key,
A clock, and a flag on a house in a tree.

I spy a horseshoe, a hammer, a ski,
A lunch box, an owl, an upside-down tee;

A squirrel, two deer, five pinecones, a mouse,
A snake, a rake, and a distant lighthouse.

I spy a fishhook, an old paper clip,

A goose, a crab, and a cloudy ship;

A fish, a nail, a pencil, an oar,
The face of a man, and an X on a door.

I spy an oilcan, two loose screws,

Two saw blades, and seven horseshoes;

I spy an oilcan, two loose screws,
Two saw blades, and seven horseshoes;

A fish, a nail, a pencil, an oar,
The face of a man, and an X on a door.

An eggshell, a nutshell, a seashell, and SOAP,
An old envelope, and a knot in a rope.

I spy a bird's nest, three spiders, a key,

A pulley, a pirate, and THINK OF ME;

A lady, a plate, an acorn cap,
Three snail shells, and another treasure map!

I spy a boot, a ruler, five jacks,

A hook, a saw, three starfish, an ax;

A skull and crossbones, a castle door,
And I'll get binoculars from page 24.

I spy a button, a walnut hull,

A bobby pin, the teeth of a skull;

A wishbone tree, a moon, a bell—
Are the teeth of the skull the stones of a well?

Hauling up treasure, I spy a note,
A camel, a leopard, a beetle, a boat;

An acorn, two lizards, a lock, and a key,
Three thimbles, three fish, five hearts: all for me!

EXTRA CREDIT RIDDLES

"Find Me" Riddle

I sit, I perch, I fly to and fro;

I'm in every picture; I'm a sleek black _____.

Find the Pictures That Go With These Riddles:

I spy a cat, a horse, and a lock,

A trapdoor, a nest, a reel, and a clock.

I spy a frog, five cats, five bees,

Four white hats, and four palm trees.

I spy a doghouse, a triangle stamp,

A birthday candle, and Aladdin's lamp.

I spy a sword, a shovel, a sail,

A dolphin, a hammer, a bottle, and WHALE.

I spy a key ring, a baseball, a horn,

A zipper pull tab, a fork, and corn.

I spy a lion, a spring, an oar,

A lobster claw, and a dinosaur.

I spy a tortoise, a teapot, a sword,

A dolphin, a shell, and a man overboard.

I spy a frog, a crown for a king,

A lantern, an owl, and a golden ring.

I spy a duck, a ruler, a broom,

A paddle, a cane, and a little mushroom.

I spy a poodle, a little red pail,

Five anchors, a cat, a duck, and a whale.

I spy a lizard, five bottles, a lock,

Shark teeth, an egg, and a fossil rock.

I spy an arrowhead, two turtles, a dog,

Antlers, a pinecone, a feather, and a frog.

How *I Spy Treasure Hunt* Was Made

I Spy Treasure Hunt is the tenth book in the I Spy series. For this book, I decided to do something different. Rather than build one set for each photograph as I did for previous I Spy books, I built a miniature village, a place called Smuggler's Cove, and photographed it from five points of view. To do this, I needed the help of an assistant and three freelance model-makers. Smuggler's Cove was built on a sixteen-by-sixteen-foot stage in HO scale (1:87). "The Treasure Chest Store," "The Map," "The Tree House and the Waterfall," "Shelter from the Storm," "The Cave," and "Treasure at Last!" were separate sets constructed at larger scales. "The Beach" was a large scale model used in combination with the HO scale landscape. All sets were photographed with a four-by-five-view camera. The entire project, from the planning and the sketches, to the completion of the sets and photographs, took nine months. All the sets were taken apart. But they live on in the photographs, in the poetry of Jean Marzollo, and in the adventure we call *I Spy Treasure Hunt*.

I would like to thank the following people for helping me build the *I Spy Treasure Hunt* sets: Daniel Helt, for his assistance with the photography and model-making throughout the entire project; Bruce Morozko for his help with model-making and set construction on "The Tree House and the Waterfall," "The Cave," "The Beach," "Shelter from the Storm," "Treasure at Last!" and background details in "Arrival" and "View from the Fort"; Michael Lokensgard for fine detail work in "Arrival," "View from Duck Pond Inn," "View from the Fort," and "Shelter from the Storm"; John Bassano for assembling and painting many of the houses and other kit models used in the village; and Linda Cheverton-Wick for artistic advice, encouragement, and support on every aspect of the project. A special thanks to Scholastic editors Grace Maccarone and Bernette Ford, and to art director Edie Weinberg for their wise advice and kind patience. Also thanks to Will Altman, Barbara Ardizone, the Goff Family, Jeff Hirsch of Foto Care Limited NYC, and Rick Schwab of Rick's Image Works NYC.

Walter Wick

Walter Wick is the photographer of the I Spy books, including *I Spy: A Book of Picture Riddles*, *I Spy Christmas*, *I Spy Fun House*, and *I Spy Spooky Night*. He is both author and photographer of *A Drop of Water: A Book of Science and Wonder*, an ALA Notable Book and winner of the Boston Globe/Horn Book Award for nonfiction, and *Walter Wick's Optical Tricks*, an ALA Notable Book, a *New York Times* Best Illustrated Book, and a Parent's Choice Silver Honor Book. Prior to creating children's books, Mr. Wick invented photographic games for *Games* magazine and photographed more than 300 covers for books and magazines, including *Newsweek*, *Discover*, and *Psychology Today*. Mr. Wick is a graduate of Paier College of Art. He lives with his wife, Linda, in New York City and Connecticut.

How to Write I Spy riddles

The I Spy books help children look at the world more carefully, use language more vividly, and think more creatively. When I visit schools, I find that many students make wonderful I Spy pictures and that they often need help with their riddles. Here's some advice: (1) Look for interesting words, such as thumbtack and hatchet. (2) Put words like shovel and shark together because they have the same initial sound; that's called alliteration. (3) Put words like crab, bats, and map together because they have the same interior sound. Look for rhymes: oar/store, key/tree, jacks/ax. Rhythm and rhyme are essential! Every I Spy line has four measures, and each measure has three beats. To test your riddles, you can sing them to an old-fashioned song, "Sweet Betsy from Pike." If you learn it, you can sing your way through I Spy!

I would like to thank the following people for helping me test this book: the kids at Riverview Elementary School in Denville, NJ, and at Martin Elementary School in Manchester, CT; Michelle, Jennifer, and Donna Cotennec; Lura, Timothy, Julia, and Jonathan Briggs; Zak Colangelo and Ben Levine; Clea Colangelo and Stefan Jimenez; Allison Thompson, Katie Brennan, and Sri Kuehnlenz; Michaela, Stephen, and Kathy Everett; Mim Galligan, Sheila Rauch, and Margaret Hare; Chris and Molly Nowak, Claudio Marzollo, and once again Dave Marzollo for his outstanding creative output.

Jean Marzollo

Jean Marzollo has written many award-winning children's books including ten I Spy picture riddle books and five I Spy Little books. She has also written *Ten Cats Have Hats; I Am Water; I Am Snow; In 1492; Happy Birthday, Martin Luther King; Pretend You're a Cat; Close Your Eyes; Home Sweet Home; Sun Song; Mama Mama; Do You Know New?; Soccer Sam;* and with her sons, Dan and Dave Marzollo, *Football Friends; Hockey Hero; Basketball Buddies;* and *Baseball Brothers.* For nineteen years, Jean Marzollo and Carol Carson produced Scholastic's kindergarten magazine, *Let's Find Out.* Ms. Marzollo holds a master's degree from the Harvard Graduate School of Education. She is director of the Vassar College Children's Book Institute of Publishing and Writing. She lives with her husband Claudio in Cold Spring, New York.

Carol Devine Carson, the book designer for the I Spy series, is art director for a major publishing house in New York City.

Other I Spy books:

I SPY: A BOOK OF PICTURE RIDDLES

New York Public Library: One Hundred Titles — For Reading and Sharing;
California Children's Media Award, Honorable Mention

I SPY CHRISTMAS: A BOOK OF PICTURE RIDDLES

Parents Magazine, Best Books List

I SPY FUN HOUSE: A BOOK OF PICTURE RIDDLES

Publishers Weekly's Best Books of 1993; American Bookseller Pick of the Lists

I SPY MYSTERY: A BOOK OF PICTURE RIDDLES

Publishers Weekly's Best Books of 1993; American Bookseller Pick of the Lists;
National Parenting Publications Award, Honorable Mention

I SPY FANTASY: A BOOK OF PICTURE RIDDLES

Book-Of-The-Month Club Main Selection

I SPY SCHOOL DAYS: A BOOK OF PICTURE RIDDLES

American Bookseller Pick of the Lists;
New York Public Library: One Hundred Titles — For Reading and Sharing

I SPY SPOOKY NIGHT: A BOOK OF PICTURE RIDDLES

Book-Of-The-Month Club Main Selection

I SPY SUPER CHALLENGER!: A BOOK OF PICTURE RIDDLES

I SPY GOLD CHALLENGER!: A BOOK OF PICTURE RIDDLES

And for the youngest child:

I SPY LITTLE BOOK

I SPY LITTLE ANIMALS

I SPY LITTLE WHEELS

I SPY LITTLE NUMBERS

I SPY LITTLE CHRISTMAS

Also available:

I SPY CD-ROM

Oppenheim Toy Portfolio Platinum Award; Home PC Reviewers' Choice Award;
Thunderbeam Best Game for Kids; Parents' Choice Seal of Approval
Bologna New Media Prize for Logic

I SPY SPOOKY MANSION CD-ROM

I SPY JUNIOR CD-ROM